Lesley Fairfield
TYRANNY

This is a work of fiction. Names, characters, places and incidents are either the product of the author's imagination or, if real, are used fictitiously. All statements, activities, stunts, descriptions, information and material of any other kind contained herein are included for entertainment purposes only and should not be relied on for accuracy or replicated as they may result in injury.

First published in Great Britain 2011 by Walker Books Ltd
87 Vauxhall Walk, London SE11 5HJ

2 4 6 8 10 9 7 5 3

This book has been typeset in Fill Meijer

Printed and bound in Great Britain by Clays Ltd, St Ives plc

British Library Cataloguing in Publication Data:
a catalogue record for this book is
available from the British Library

ISBN 978-1-4063-3113-4

www.walker.co.uk

To Raymond,
who convinced me
that this book was possible.

ACKNOWLEDGEMENTS

Thanks to Joan Fairfield, for understanding. I'm grateful to Diana Abraham for typing the script at lightning speed, and Tony Fairfield for his computer savvy. Thanks to Mike and Jan, Ken, Ed, Dom, Kat, Christine, Gabriel, Eva Mae, Katie and Isabel for inspiration.

My gratitude to Peter Garstang for help when I needed it most, to Margaret McBurney for her encouragement, and to Plum Johnson for her kindness and generosity.

To my consultant and psychiatrist Dr Helen Mesaros, my Dr Moon, who helped me realize my dream to be an artist again.

Special thanks to my agent Samantha Haywood for her knowledge and experience in the development of this book. I'm grateful to Kathryn Cole for her good humour and intuitive editing, to Katie Everson for her cover design and wonderful eye, to Kathy Lowinger and Lizzie Spratt for their confidence in me, and to Paul Kelly for showing me the magic of Photoshop.

And to all the girls in this story who haunt me, still.

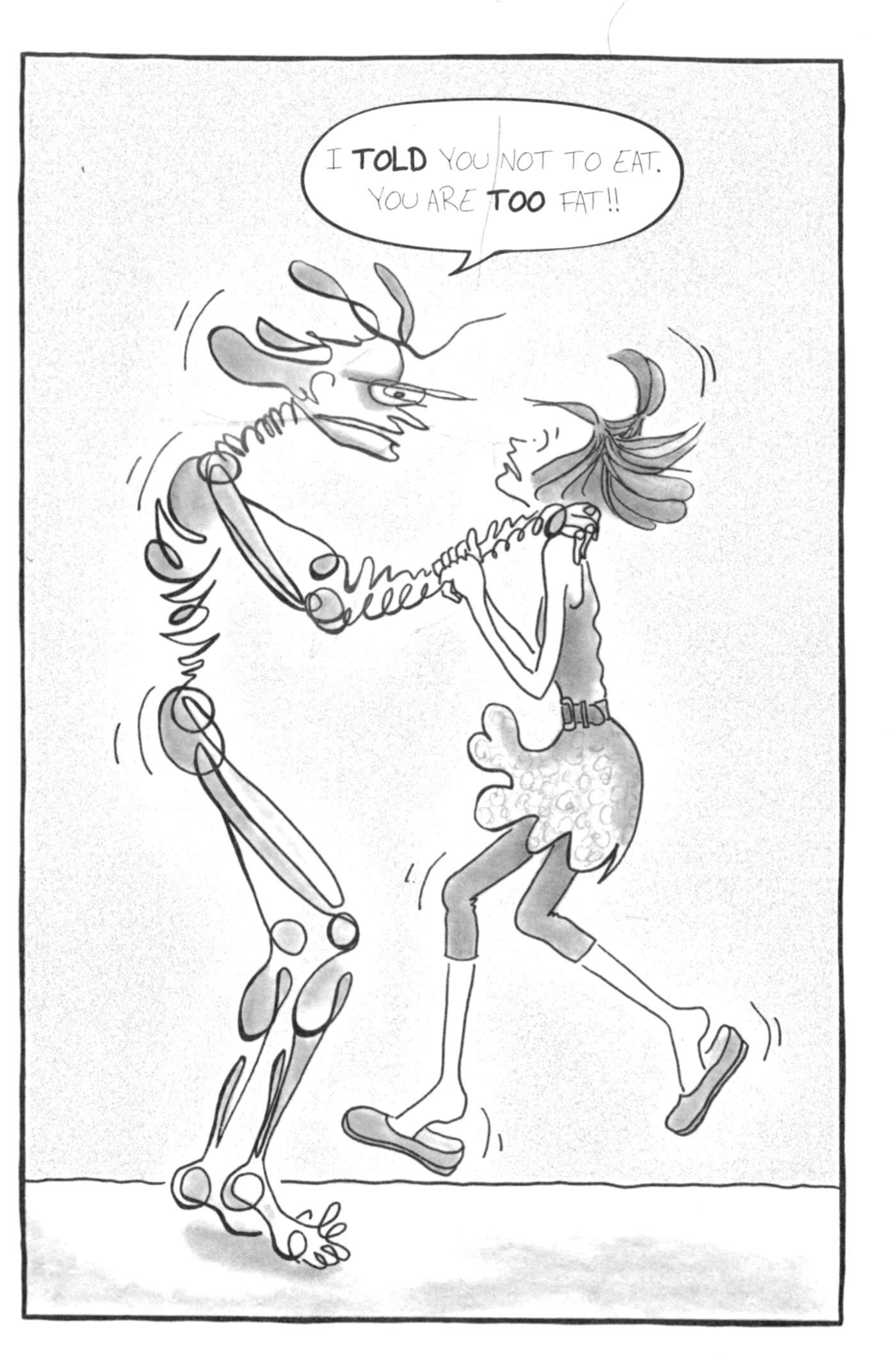
I TOLD YOU NOT TO EAT.
YOU ARE TOO FAT!!

I'VE GOT TO TRY!!
GASP
NO, YOU DON'T!

YOU'LL **RUIN** YOUR LIFE!!
BUT HOW CAN I LIVE AND NOT EAT?

HOW DID I GET TO THIS PLACE?

IT USED TO BE DIFFERENT. NOTHING BOTHERED ME. I WAS REALLY EXCITED ABOUT THE FUTURE. I HAD SO MANY QUESTIONS.
Will I be beautiful?
Will I be happy?
Who will I love?
Will he love me?
How many children will I have? Quite a few I hope.
Will we have a dog?
How old will I be when I die? Will anyone miss me?
But I don't want to die.
Isn't it amazing that I exist?
SPACE
ME
EARTH
What will my house be like?
TOWER
GREEN ROOF
WATER SLIDE
POND
Will my work be thrilling?
I love spaghetti VERY much.
I wonder what's for dinner?

WHAT I WANTED MOST WAS TO BECOME A WRITER. MY MIND WAS FULL OF STORIES. I WAS SO IMMERSED IN THEM, I HARDLY NOTICED ANYTHING ELSE.
ANNA!
ANNA!
ANNA!
DINNER'S READY!
A-A-N-N-N-A!
GET DOWN FROM THERE!
ANNA!
ANNA!
JUST A MINUTE.
MY HAT!
THEN, I SWAM FROM ICEBERG TO ICEBERG.
TO DINE, OR NOT TO DINE?
IT'S ANNA'S MUM!
GO AWAY!
WHY, OH WHY, OH WHY, OH WHY?
WOW.
IN WINTER, TOO.
GASP!
EW.
A PERFECT DRESS!
VERY NICE.
SURE.
DANCE?
DARLING!
SO, WHERE'S THE CAR?
I FORGET.
UH-OH!
WE'VE GOT TO HURRY!
– AGAIN?
ARE WE LATE –
LOVELY!
YOU WON?
YUP.
and then . . .

BUT THINGS BEGAN TO CHANGE . . .

TIME PASSED...
Mirrors Don't Lie
I HATE THIS!
I REALLY HATE THIS!
Mirrors Don't Lie
I REALLY, REALLY HATE THIS!
MUM!!
Mirrors Don't Lie

YOU'RE NOT TOO BIG! STOP WORRYING, SWEETIE. THIS IS ALL A VERY NORMAL PART OF GROWING UP.
BUT IT LOOKS LIKE FAT TO ME, MUM!
WELL IT'S NOT, DEAR. JUST BE CAREFUL YOU DON'T GAIN TOO MUCH MORE WEIGHT.
OH.
MY DAD STOPPED HUGGING ME.
I'M JUST TRYING TO GIVE YOU SPACE, HONEY.
I MISUNDERSTOOD.

I FELT TRAPPED INSIDE MY NEW BODY.
MY IMAGINATION WORKED OVERTIME, AND BEFORE LONG,
I WAS TORMENTED AND MISERABLE!
I HATE THIS.
I HATE ME!

I WAS DESPERATE TO HAVE MY YOUNGER BODY BACK.
LET ME OUT!

I DECIDED TO GO ON A DIET. I WENT TO THE BOOKSHOP, AND BEGAN TO READ . . .

I RESTRICTED MY EATING FOR WEEKS, AND SOON . . .

I WAS PLEASED WITH MY SLENDER SELF. I GAVE ALL MY OLD CLOTHES AWAY TO MY FRIENDS...

I LECTURED THEM ABOUT FOOD...

I WENT SHOPPING AND SPENT MY SAVINGS ON A NEW WARDROBE.
AMAZING!

AS LONG AS I'M THIN AND PERFECT . . .

. . . I'LL BE INVINCIBLE!

IN MY MEDIA CLASS . . .
Leonardo da Vinci's 'Vitruvian Man'
I'D LIKE YOU TO TAKE A LOOK AT THIS STUDY IN HUMAN PROPORTION. WHEN THE LIMBS ARE OUTSTRETCHED, THE BODY WILL FORM A PERFECT CIRCLE, WITH THE BELLY BUTTON AT THE VERY CENTRE. LET'S SEE WHAT HAPPENS WHEN WE APPLY LEONARDO'S FORMULA TO A DIGITALLY ALTERED PHOTOGRAPH. ALTHOUGH SHAPES AND SIZES VARY IN THE REAL WORLD, LET ME SHOW YOU THE FASHION INDUSTRY STANDARD.
THIS MODEL'S SHAPE HAS BEEN ADJUSTED FOR PUBLICATION. HER ARMS ARE NOW MUCH TOO SHORT PROPORTIONALLY, AND DON'T MATCH HER LEGS. THIS MODERN IDEAL IS AN ILLUSION, AND, AS SUCH, IS UNATTAINABLE. USE AN ANALYTICAL EYE WHEN YOU LOOK AT A FASHION MAGAZINE PHOTO AND GIRLS, REMEMBER, THE MOST BEAUTIFUL YOU IS YOU.
Modern Model
LEO'S CIRCLE
LEO'S CIRCLE
LEO'S CIRCLE
FASHION CIRCLE
MUM SAYS THAT ALL THE TIME. HOW LAME!
KIND OF INTERESTING.
YEAH.
HMM.

ONE DAY AFTER CLASS . . .
HEY.
HEY.
I NEVER NOTICED YOU BEFORE.
I WAS HIDING.
MY NAME'S TIM. WHAT'S YOURS?
ANNA.
I LIKE YOUR SMILE.
THANKS.
CAN I WALK YOU HOME?
OK.

I LIKED TIM SO MUCH, AND WE STARTED GOING OUT TOGETHER. I WAS SURE HE'D HATE IT IF I GAINED WEIGHT.
THIS IS A GREAT BURGER!
THIS SALAD IS GOOD TOO.
WANT A BITE?
OH, NO. NO, NO!
THANKS.

MY PARENTS WORRIED.
SHE IS SO BOSSY.
I DIDN'T WANT TO EAT, EVEN WHEN I WAS HUNGRY.
I DON'T WANT ANYTHING! I CAN'T!
I HID MY BODY FROM MY MOTHER IN SECONDHAND DUNGAREES.
GO AWAY!

WHEN MY PARENTS WEREN'T LOOKING . . .

I STARTED TO WEIGH MYSELF SEVERAL TIMES A DAY.
98!
FATSO
98?
AGAIN?
FATSO
98 1/2!
FATSO
IS THIS ADJUSTED PROPERLY?
WHAT DID I DO WRONG?
STILL TOO HEAVY.
I WON'T GO OUT WITH TIM AGAIN UNTIL I'M 97 POUNDS.
97!
TIM!

THAT JULY, I WENT BACK TO MY JOB AS A CAMP COUNSELLOR. BUT THAT SUMMER WAS DIFFERENT FROM THE OTHERS. ONE DAY, I WAS PADDLING MY CANOE . . .

I WON'T EAT I WON'T
WON'T WON'T EAT
I WON EAT I W
I WO EAT WON
I W I WO
EA EAT I WO
E T I W

CLICK!

I WILL EAT I WILL EAT
I WILL I WILL EAT I
I WILL I WILL
I WILL I WILL
I WILL EAT I
EAT I WILL E
WILL EAT

I WILL EAT EVERYTHING
NUTS
COOKIES
DOUGHNUTS
CHIPS
CANDY
JAM
CAKE
BUTTER

LATER . . .

WHAT HAVE I DONE?
EATING ISN'T FATAL, ANNA.
FREUD WOULD LOVE THIS!
WOULDN'T HE?
I HAVE A HALF-BRAIN I DIDN'T KNOW ABOUT AND IT CONTRADICTS THE OTHER HALF. THERE'S A SWITCH BETWEEN THEM. ONE HALF SAYS "NO" AND THE OTHER HALF SAYS "YES!"
My Brain
Switch is usually here
But it clicked over to here
No control
Control
AND I DON'T KNOW WHO FLICKED THE SWITCH.

SCHOOL STARTED IN SEPTEMBER, AND TIM AND I WERE REUNITED.
TIM!
ANNA!
I MISSED YOU!
I MISSED YOU!
LOOK! WE'VE GOT SOME OF THE SAME CLASSES!
GREAT!
COOL.
SO COOL!

BUT SOON SCHOOL WAS TOO MUCH FOR ME. I ATE LESS AND LESS.
I DON'T HAVE TO EAT. NO, I DON'T!
I'LL JUST DRINK COFFEE! IT WILL FILL ME UP.
GLUB GLUB GLUB GLUB
TIM NOTICED HOW THIN I WAS, AND STARTED TO QUESTION ME.
WHAT'S WRONG, ANNA? I THOUGHT YOU LOVED SPAGHETTI!
I . . . I . . . JUST CAN'T EAT THIS, TIM.

I SPENT MORE AND MORE TIME IN MY ROOM, TALKING TO MYSELF.

ANNA, I'M WORRIED ABOUT YOU. YOU DON'T HAVE ANOREXIA, DO YOU?
GASP!
THERE'S NOTHING WRONG WITH ME!
WHY CAN'T YOU ACCEPT ME THE WAY I AM?

I COULD NO LONGER CONCENTRATE, AND FELL FAR BEHIND IN CLASSES. I DROPPED OUT OF SCHOOL ON VALENTINE'S DAY.
I FELT AS IF I HAD BEEN WALKING A TIGHTROPE.
AND HAD FALLEN OFF . . .
N-O-O-O-O-O

AND WAS AT THE BEGINNING OF A LONG DESCENT.

I COULDN'T LIVE AT HOME ANY MORE. MY PARENTS' WORRYING WAS DRIVING ME CRAZY. I HAD SOME MONEY SAVED AND MOVED TO A FURNISHED FLAT NEARBY. I PROMISED TO PHONE MY MOTHER EVERY DAY, BUT I DIDN'T.
DID I DIE?
Love. Tim
Silence
FRAGILE
Silence
MY LIFE IS GONE
BUT
I'M ALIVE
AND
I'M DEAD TOO.
CLICK!

LATER . . .
CHIPS
I FAILED I ATE I FA
TE I FAILED I ATE I
ATE I FAILED I ATE
I FAILED
FAILED
FAILED
FAILED
RING
ANNA, CAN I SEE YOU?
NOT NOW, TIM. FRIDAY?
OK THEN, FRIDAY. BYE.
SEE YOU THEN. BYE.
Monday
I JUST CAN'T LET HIM SEE ME BLOATED
LIKE THIS.
Wednesday
AS LONG AS I DON'T EAT, I'LL LOOK BETTER
BY FRIDAY.
Friday
BETTER -
WITH MAKEUP.

ON FRIDAY NIGHT . . .
I CARE ABOUT YOU, ANNA.
TIM!
I'VE DONE EVERYTHING I CAN THINK OF TO HELP.
HUH?
WHAT DO YOU MEAN?
I MEAN, YOU JUST KEEP FADING AWAY, AND . . .
I DON'T KNOW WHO YOU ARE ANY MORE!
TIM, ARE . . .
ARE YOU BREAKING UP WITH ME?
YES.
GOODBYE, ANNA.
CLICK

TIM, COME BACK.
TIM?
NO! OH, NO!
TIMMMMMM!
I CRIED AND CRIED UNTIL . . .
HE'LL BE BACK.
NO, HE WON'T.
YES, HE WILL!
NO. NO, HE WON'T.
EVER!
. . . I RAN OUT OF STEAM.

I SLEPT FOR TWENTY-FOUR HOURS.
Love Tim
WHEN I AWOKE . . .
I WILL NOT EAT.
EVER, EVER AGAIN.
LATER THAT DAY . . .
I CAN'T EAT, ANYWAY. I'M BROKE.
I'VE GOT TO GET A – OH!
Sad Café
UNIQUE WAITRESS WANTED. WILL TRAIN
Queen Street Gem

I MET THE MANAGER . . .
WELL! YOU HAVE JUST THE LOOK WE WANT!
THANK YOU, HERB.
I'D LIKE YOU TO MEET THE OTHERS. CAN YOU START RIGHT AWAY?
AH . . . UM . . .
OK.
LADIES, THIS IS ANNA!
BRENDA.
DOT.
STELLA.

I MADE THE JOB MY OWN.
YOU WANTED THE LAMB?
MY STRUCTURED ROUTINE HELPED ME TO EAT MORE AT HOME . . .
Breakfast
Boiled Egg
Rye Cracker
One Orange
Black Coffee
Lunch
Apple
Black Coffee
Dinner
Two Boiled Eggs
Rye Cracker
Apple
Black Coffee
Celery
Sugarless Gum
Black Coffee
Black Coffee
Diet Drinks
. . . AS LONG AS IT WASN'T FATTENING.

I TRIED TO EAT IN THE STAFF ROOM AT THE CAFÉ, BUT JUST COULDN'T OPEN MY MOUTH, ESPECIALLY IN FRONT OF THE OTHER GIRLS.
OW!
I LOVE MEATBALLS. DON'T YOU?
JUST COFFEE FOR ME.
SQUISH!
AND CHIPS FOR ME.
SLIP
SLOBBER
ALTHOUGH THEY LOOK A LITTLE BIT STALE.
I DON'T THINK THIS IS COOKED.

I HAD JUST LEFT WORK AND WAS ON MY WAY HOME WHEN . . .
WHOAA! ANNA!
GASP!

DO I KNOW YOU?
YOU'VE ALWAYS KNOWN ME, SILLY!
I'M TYRANNY, YOUR OTHER SELF. I KEEP YOU THIN.
DON'T I LOOK FAMILIAR?
I . . . I GUESS SO.
GOOD. I THINK IT'S TIME WE HAD A TALK. YOU'RE A FATTY!
IF I COULD JUST LOSE FIVE MORE POUNDS . . .
YOU'LL LOSE THEM. DON'T YOU WORRY, SWEETIE.

I REALIZED I'D COME FACE TO FACE WITH A FORCE DEEP WITHIN MYSELF THAT WAS NO LONGER HIDING.

AWWW . . . YOU'RE MY VERY BEST FRIEND.
FROM THEN ON, WE WENT EVERYWHERE TOGETHER.
NO FOOD TODAY!!
SOON, I WEIGHED NO MORE THAN EIGHTY-FIVE POUNDS.
WHAT IF I STARVE TO DEATH?
DON'T BE SILLY. DIETING'S NOT GOING TO KILL YOU. DON'T BE SUCH A SISSY!

WELL, WHAT IF I DIE FROM BINGE EATING?
GEEEZ
DO YOU KNOW WHO CONTROLS THE SWITCH IN MY BRAIN?
YUP.
YOU DO!
NO! IT CAN'T BE ME!
I WANT TO KNOW WHAT MAKES ME DIET AND THEN BINGE LIKE THAT!
IF YOU INSIST, CRYBABY.
LET'S SEE, HERE IT IS.
TYRANNY'S BOOK OF THE TRUTH
BINGE EATING RESULTS WHEN SAID "EATER" HAS A COMPLETE LACK OF WILLPOWER, SELF CONTROL, AND DISCIPLINE!
OH.

WHERE DO I GET THE DISCIPLINE I NEED?
FROM ME!
THAT'S WHY I'M HERE!
I'LL GIVE YOU WILLPOWER, DISCIPLINE, COURAGE.
OK.
BUT STOP THINKING ABOUT FOOD!
SORRY.
LATER . . .
I'LL THINK ABOUT TIME PASSING, INSTEAD.

SAD
EMPTY
LONELY
WHO WOULD WANT ME, ANYWAY?
WHAT IF I DIE TONIGHT?
STOP IT! GO TO SLEEP!
BOSSY
THAT NIGHT, I HAD A DREAM.

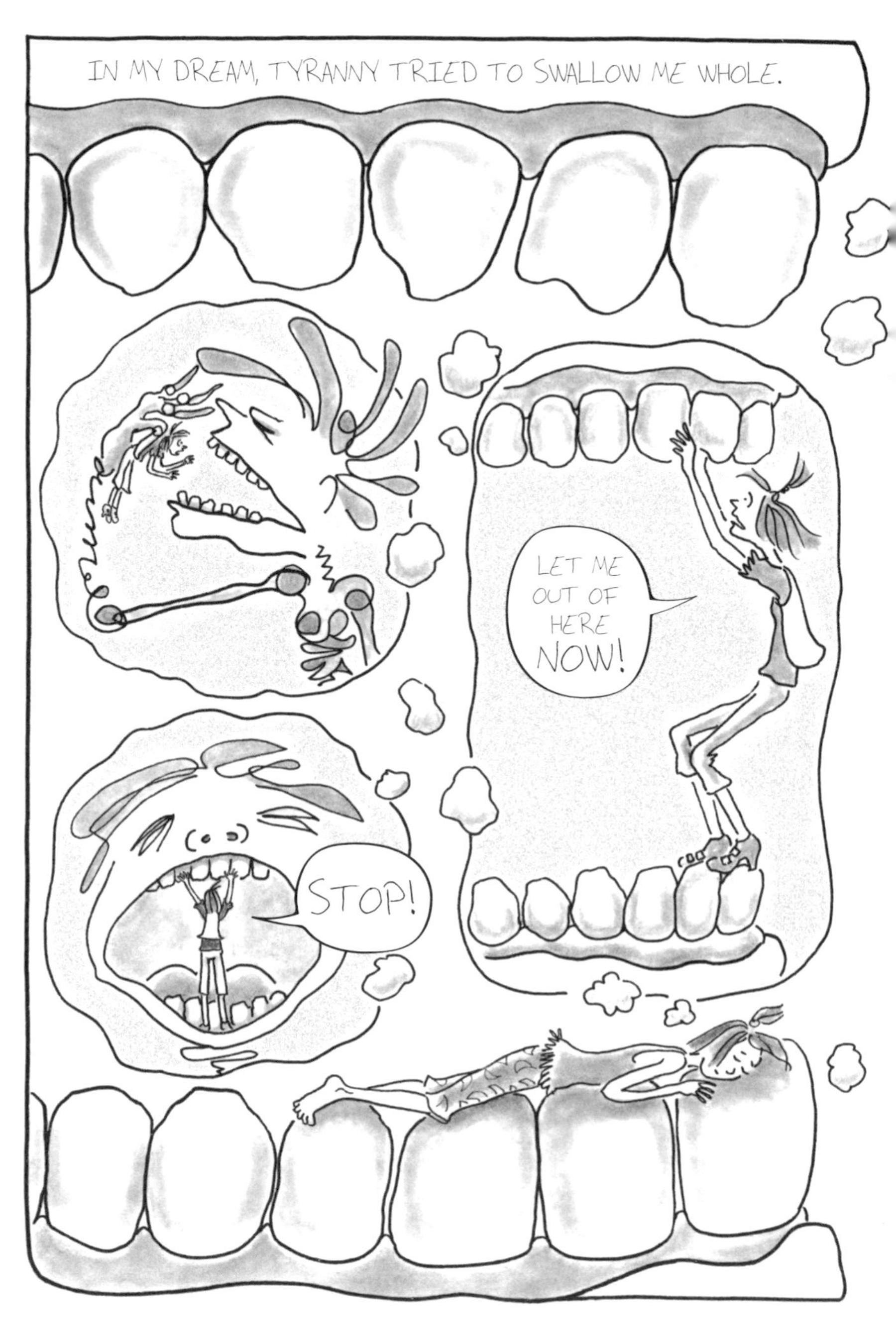
IN MY DREAM, TYRANNY TRIED TO SWALLOW ME WHOLE.
LET ME OUT OF HERE NOW!
STOP!

OW!
HEY!
I RAN . . .

. . . AND RAN . . .
. . . AND RAN . . .
. . . UNTIL I WOKE UP.
I NEVER WANT TO DREAM AGAIN.
BUT TWO NIGHTS LATER I HAD ANOTHER.

SOME DAY, SKINNY ANNA, YOU WILL BE BIG, JUST LIKE ME!
NO NO NO NO NO NO NO NO NO NO NO NO
No No NO No No

PANT PANT
I'M TRAPPED, NO MATTER WHAT I DO! I'LL NEVER ESCAPE!
I DON'T CARE.
NO, I DON'T.
CLICK!
I'M GOING TO EAT EVERYTHING I'M GOING TO EAT EVERYTHING I'M GOING TO EAT
SANDWICHES
CHOCOLATES
CAKES
GASP
PIZZA
CHIPS
TYRANNY WILL KILL ME NOW.

TICK
TICK
TICK
TICK
TICK
TICK
TAKE OUT
TICK
TICK
TICK
TICK
TICK
I WISH MY....
TICK
THUMP
THUMP
HEART WOULD...
TICK
THUMP
THUMP
THUMP
STOP POUNDING...
TICK
THUMP
THUMP
THUMP
THUMP
SO FAST!
I CAN'T BREATHE.
I'VE GOT TO LIE DOWN.

HOW COULD YOU? YOU'VE GOT TO THROW IT ALL UP!
I'M SORRY!
COME ON! STICK YOUR FINGER DOWN YOUR THROAT!
I CAN'T! I CAN'T DO IT!
YOU'VE GOT TO DO SOMETHING. YOU CAN'T JUST LEAVE THAT STUFF IN THERE. YOU'LL GET FAT!
WE'RE GOING TO GET SOME LAXATIVES - NOW!

LATER . . .
IT SAYS THIS WILL TAKE EFFECT OVERNIGHT. THAT'S GOOD. I'M NOT WORKING TOMORROW.
YUCKO
HOW MANY SHOULD I TAKE?
YUCKO
AS MANY AS I CAN!
THE NEXT MORNING, AND ALL THE NEXT DAY . . .
OW OW
CRAMPS
PAIN
NAUSEA
GAG
SHIVER
THUMP THUMP
MORNING
AFTERNOON
EVENING
HOW AM I GOING TO KEEP WORKING?
IT FEELS SO AWFUL.
MY HEART IS POUNDING AGAIN AND I'M REALLY THIRSTY.
BUT LOOK AT ME!
IT'S ALL SO WORTH IT.
ALL THE PUFFINESS IS GONE AND I'M SO GORGEOUS!

I FELL INTO A CYCLE OF BINGING AND PURGING THAT LASTED FOR MONTHS. IT WENT LIKE THIS . . . AGAIN AND AGAIN AND AGAIN.

I HOPED NO ONE IN THE REAL WORLD COULD TELL.
• Bolts Couturier • Bolts Couturier • Bolts Couturier •
NO ONE KNOWS
NO ONE KNOWS
NO
NO ONE
NO
NO ONE KNOWS
NO ONE
NO
ONE
NO
KNOWS
NO ONE
NO
ONE
NO
ONE
KNOWS
NO ONE KNOWS
NO ONE KNOWS
NO
NO ONE KNOWS
NO ONE
NO ONE
NO

IT WAS BECOMING HARDER TO HIDE MY SUFFERING AT THE CAFÉ.

ON MY WAY HOME FROM WORK ONE FRIDAY NIGHT . . .

I MADE MY WAY TO A PUBLIC WASHROOM . . .
COME ON NOW, ANNA. WE'VE BEEN HERE FOR A WHOLE HOUR. COME ON, GET UP!
. . . AND FINALLY HOME.
I WANT TO LIVE. I WANT TO LIVE. I WANT TO LIVE. I WANT TO LIVE. I WANT TO LIVE.
HOT WATER BOTTLE

THE NEXT MORNING, I HAD A VISITOR.
WHO IS IT?
HONEY, IT'S YOUR MUM!
OH!
SWEETHEART? ANNA! WHY HAVEN'T YOU ANSWERED MY CALLS?
OPEN THE DOOR!
OH, ANNA.
I'M GOING TO CALL THE DOCTOR RIGHT NOW!
OK.

AS SOON AS I WAS HOSPITALIZED, MY ANXIETY ABATED.
GO AWAY!
TAP TAP
TAP TAP
THUMP
TICK
TICK
TICK
I'M SO TIRED.
EVERYTHING'S SORE, EVEN MY SKIN.
AT LEAST I FEEL SAFE - FOR NOW.
I WAS GIVEN A MEAL PLAN, AND TRIED TO FOLLOW IT.
FEAR
NO
ANXIETY
NO
NO
NO
RELUCTANCE
SUSPICION
NO
NO
NO
PANIC
ANGER
NO
NO
NO
NO
TERROR

I MET OTHER PATIENTS.
HI, I'M ANNA.
ELAINE.
MEG.
SANDY.
YVONNE.

I STARTED SEEING A PSYCHIATRIST, NAMED DR MOON.
I DIDN'T REALLY WANT TO GO, BUT WHEN I DID . . .
YES. IF THAT WAS YOUR FEELING, THAT WAS YOUR FEELING.
YOU CAN LEARN TO CLAIM YOUR THOUGHTS.
BUT, ARE THEY REALLY ME, OR WHAT I THINK THEY SHOULD BE?
FINDING THE REAL YOU IS WHAT WE'RE DOING HERE.
WHERE DID I GO?

I REALIZED I WAS BEING NURTURED IN A WAY I HAD NOT BEEN ABLE TO DO FOR MYSELF. I WAS TAKEN BACK TO THE BEGINNING, TO REBUILD MYSELF FROM THE GROUND UP. IT WAS A LONG, AND SOMETIMES TEDIOUS, PROCESS.
LOVE OF LIFE
AWARENESS OF SELF-DEFEATING BEHAVIOURS AND STRATEGIES TO AVOID REPEATING THEM
NOT TOO FAST, ANNA.
THERAPY
DON'T GIVE UP
ACCEPT WHAT CAN'T BE CHANGED; CHANGE THINGS THAT CAN BE CHANGED
WRITING, IDEAS, PLAYS, LYRICS, JOURNALS, STORIES
RECOGNIZE PEOPLE'S PLEASING BEHAVIOURS
THIS ABOVE ALL ELSE; TO THINE OWN SELF BE TRUE. — HAMLET
P.S. FIND OUT WHO SELF IS
FUN DANCE FRIENDS DANCE MUSIC
LIFE PLAN
TREES SUMMER CAMP CANOES
FOLLOW FOOD PLAN. FOOD IS GOOD.
EDUCATION: ACADEMIC AND OTHERWISE
TRUST YOUR OWN THOUGHTS
LOVE AND SAFETY
SELF NURTURE
BOOKS AND READING

I WORKED HARD WITH DR MOON, AND BEGAN TO MAKE SOME DECISIONS ABOUT MY LIFE.
IF I COULD JUST GET A JOB THAT WOULD USE MY WRITING . . .
I DOUBT THAT!
HONEST ADVERTISING CORPORATION. HAC WANTS YOU. THIS IS INTERESTING!
HACK
HACK
WILL TRAIN!
WELL WHOOP DEE DOO!
I WENT FOR AN INTERVIEW.
HAC
WE'D LIKE TO HIRE YOU. CAN YOU START MONDAY?
OF COURSE! THANK YOU.
I'M PICKING UP THE PIECES OF MY LIFE.
NOT SO FAST.

YOU CAN'T START WORK LIKE THIS! YOU'RE WAY TOO FAT FAT FAT FAT!!
CLICK
CLICK
CLICK
LAXATI
EAT LA
LAXAT
EAT L
LAXA
EAT LA
LAXATIV
LAXATIVES
LAXATIVES
THE NEXT DAY . . .
I'VE GOT TO GO SHOPPING. I HOPE I CAN MAKE IT.
I NEED NEW STUFF FOR WORK. BUT I TOOK
TOO MANY LAXATIVES AND I'M SO WEAK.
I'LL SHOP . . .
GASP . . .
VERY SLOWLY.
DIZZY
SIGH
WEAK
THUMP
FAT
THUMP
THIRSTY
WHAT'S THAT?
THUMPITY
THUMPITY
THUMPITY
THUMPITY
THUMP
THUMP

I'LL JUST IGNORE IT.
MIND OVER MATTER.
FEAR FEAR FEAR FEAR FEAR FEAR FEAR FEAR FEAR FEAR FEAR FEAR FEAR FEAR FEAR FEAR FEAR FEAR FEAR FEAR FEAR FEAR FEAR
DRIFT
BUT NATURE IS TELLING ME SOMETHING.
I'VE GOT TO LISTEN!
THUMP THUMP THUMP THUMP

AM I DYING?
I DON'T WANT TO DIE! IT'S TOO SOON!
LET ME LIVE.
LET ME LIVE.
LET ME LIVE.
I WAITED, AND AN HOUR LATER . . .
LET ME LIVE.
. . . I WALKED SLOWLY HOME.

POP
WONK
BLANK
FOG
HAZE
THE FOLLOWING DAY, I STARTED MY NEW JOB BUT FOUND THAT I COULDN'T CONCENTRATE. IT DIDN'T SEEM TO MATTER, BECAUSE NONE OF THE OTHER GIRLS THERE COULD CONCENTRATE EITHER.
CYNTHIA
ESTHER
MONIQUE
BILLY

WE HAD A LOT IN COMMON AND WENT TO LUNCH EVERY DAY.
SO, ANNA, WHAT DO YOU REALLY WANT TO DO?
SHE ALWAYS ASKS.
DO?
WHAT SHE MEANS, IS, WHAT'S YOUR PASSION?
I'M A DANCER.
UNDECIDED.
OH, I WANT TO WRITE.
I MODEL.
SHE'S OUR CELEBRITY.
DANCING FREES ME.
LOVELY.
I'M TRYING TO FIND MY MUSE.
I'M FASHION'S MUSE.
YUM.

NO ONE LOVES ME FOR ME.
ME NEITHER.
OH, LOVE.
I'D HAVE TO LOSE WEIGHT.
ME TOO.
WANT A MUFFIN?
NO THANKS.
WHO NEEDS FOOD?
NOT US!
I HAVE TO DIET FOR MODELLING.
I DIET FOR DANCING.
I'M TRYING TO EAT.
I CAN'T STOP!
WINE'S MY FOOD.

ESTHER ASKED US TO ATTEND HER EATING DISORDER GROUP.
YOU'RE NOT ALONE. DON'T GIVE UP. YOU CAN DO IT. STAY HONEST.
I FEEL SO INVISIBLE.
ME TOO.
TRY HARDER! GO EASY. BE REAL.
LOVE
LOVE
LOVE
LOVE
LOVE
LOVE
LOVE
LOVE
AFTERWARDS . . .
I THINK THEY'RE SCARY.
OH, NO! I THINK THEY'RE BRAVE!
I GUESS WE SHOULD JOIN . . . SOMETIME.
I THOUGHT IT WAS VERY POWERFUL.
GOOD.
We're All the Same

BUT INSTEAD OF GOING TO MEETINGS, WE WENT JOGGING.
GASP
WHEEZE

AND WE WENT SHOPPING.
BORING
TOO BIG
TOO PRICEY
TOO SMALL
IS THAT A ZERO ZERO?
TRANSPARENT! WOW!
70% OFF.
HMMM.

BUT THE MORE CLOTHES WE TRIED ON . . .

I HATE MY HUGE THIGHS.
AND MY BIG BUM.
LOOK AT MY CHUNKY KNEES.
MINE TOO.
THESE WOULD LOOK SO PRETTY IN A SMALLER SIZE . . .
IF IT WEREN'T FOR MY BIG FAT FEET.
YEAH.

DOES THIS MAKE ME LOOK FAT?

WE WENT TO ALL OF CYNTHIA'S FASHION SHOWS.

CYNTHIA BECAME MY CLOSEST FRIEND.
I'M SO DEPRESSED. MY AGENT SAYS I HAVE TO LOSE WEIGHT.
BUT YOU'RE THIN ALREADY.
SHE DOESN'T THINK SO.
WANT TO MEET ME TOMORROW? WE COULD GO SHOPPING.
SURE.
WE MET FOR A LATE LUNCH.
NO MATTER HOW HARD I TRY, I'LL NEVER BE GOOD ENOUGH.
NOT TRUE, CYN!

AND LOOK.
NOW MY HAIR'S FALLING OUT!
AND THE ENAMEL ON MY TEETH IS ERODING.
WELL, MINE IS, BUT YOU'RE STILL BEAUTIFUL.
DO YOU KNOW WHAT I HAVE TO DO TO STAY BEAUTIFUL?
OH, CYN.
I THROW UP ALL THE TIME. NOW I CAN'T STOP THROWING UP, EVEN WHEN I DON'T WANT TO!

WHAT DOES YOUR DOCTOR SAY?
NOTHING. I HAVEN'T TOLD HER.

CYNTHIA HAD BEEN AWAY FROM WORK FOR SEVERAL DAYS.

DO YOU THINK . . . IS SHE GOING TO PAY HER RENT?
I – DON'T – KNOW!
WHEN I VISITED HER IN THE HOSPITAL, CYNTHIA SEEMED VERY FAR AWAY.
LOVE YOU, CYN. YOU'LL MAKE IT. I KNOW YOU WILL.
BUT CYNTHIA DIDN'T MAKE IT. SHE DIED A WEEK LATER. THE PORTRAITS FROM HER MODELLING PORTFOLIO WERE ALL THAT WAS LEFT, AND THEY WEREN'T CYNTHIA AT ALL.

To thine own self be true
I SHOULD HAVE FORCED HER TO GET HELP.
YUCKO
I FAILED HER AND I MISS HER.
WHAT A WASTE OF A LIFE.
I'M JUST THE SAME, EXCEPT I'M THE LIVING DEAD!
WHO CARES? JUST DON'T BE FAT!

I HAD NEVER FELT SO LOST. I TRIED TO REMEMBER WHO I WAS, BUT ALL I COULD THINK ABOUT WAS . . .
I WON'T BE FAT.
I WON'T BE . . .
I WON'T . . .
I . . .
I . . . ?
I . . . ?
I . . . ?
I . . . ?

AT DR MOON'S . . .
HOW DO YOU FEEL ABOUT WHAT HAPPENED TO CYNTHIA?
I'M SAD AND REALLY SCARED.
ARE YOU AFRAID IT COULD HAPPEN TO YOU?
YEAH.
DR MOON TOLD ME SOMETHING I WOULD REMEMBER FOR A LONG TIME.
ANNA, WHEN YOU SLIP BACKWARDS, YOU'LL NEVER FALL BACK TO THE VERY BEGINNING. IF YOU KEEP TRYING, YOU'LL GET THERE.
COME ON, ANNA! FIGHT FOR YOURSELF. FIGHT!

BUT TYRANNY AND LAXATIVES OVERWHELMED ME. ONE DAY, NOT FAR FROM THE OFFICE, I STOPPED.

SWEETHEART?
ARE YOU ALL RIGHT?

I HAVE A GRANDDAUGHTER ABOUT YOUR AGE. DID YOU FAINT?
UMM.
I'LL GET YOU SOME WATER.
OK.
YOU JUST SIT FOR A BIT, DEAR. YOU'RE MUCH TOO THIN.
I . . . I . . . KNOW.
I'LL CALL YOU A CAB. WHEN YOU GET HOME, EAT SOMETHING. YOU ARE A LOVELY YOUNG GIRL, AND YOU MUST TAKE CARE OF YOURSELF.
SOB

LATER...
I WONDER IF THAT LADY KNEW? IT DOESN'T MATTER IF SHE DID - A COMPLETE STRANGER HAD MORE COMPASSION FOR ME THAN I DO FOR MYSELF.
COMPASSION WILL MAKE YOU FAT!!
WHAT IF SOME THINGS ARE MORE IMPORTANT THAN BEING THIN?
ARE YOU CRAZY?
MAYBE I'M NOT.

AT DR MOON'S . . .
THERAPY CAN BE JUST LIKE WHITE WATER RAFTING.
WHEN YOU BECOME TOO FOCUSED ON THE ROCKS . . .
. . . I TRY TO NUDGE YOU AROUND THEM, AND OUT INTO OPEN WATER.

I WANT TO BE IN OPEN WATER!
I KNOW. AND I THINK YOU NEED THAT FINAL NUDGE.
O . . . . OK.
I HAVE A TREATMENT CENTRE IN MIND WITH AN INTENSIVE PROGRAMME THAT WILL COMPLEMENT THE WORK YOU'VE DONE SO FAR WITH ME. I CAN BOOK YOU IN FRIDAY EVENING.
FRIDAY? I'LL HAVE TO QUIT MY JOB. I . . . . I'LL . . . . I'LL DO IT! I'LL GO!
DON'T GO!
DON'T GO!
DON'T GO!
DON'T GO!
DON'T GO!
DON'T GO!
I'M GOING AND THAT'S THAT!

THAT FRIDAY NIGHT . . .
HI JOAN.
HI ANNA.
JOAN
HI.
STAFF
S M T
BREAKFAST SHIFT
LUNCH SHIFT
DINNER SHIFT
EATING DISORDERS UNIT
EAST WING
HERE'S ANOTHER ONE.
SHE'S SO THIN.
LATER . . .
ANNA, THIS IS YOUR ROOMMATE, LILY.
HI.
HI.
SO WHEN DO WE HAVE TO GET UP?
6:45
YIKES!
YEAH, BUT IT'S GOOD HERE.
I COULDN'T SLEEP AT FIRST.
IT FEELS LIKE A PRISON AND A REFUGE AT THE SAME TIME. I WONDER WHAT WILL HAPPEN?
CAN'T YOU GUESS?

THE NEXT MORNING, I READ THE RULES.

Welcome, welcome, welcome, welcome.

RULES

1. Eat every meal.
2. Remain at the table until everyone has finished eating.
3. Eat all of every meal provided.
4. No unsupervised trips to washroom.
5. Remain in building unless permission to leave is granted.
6. No food other than that provided.
7. No visitors without permission.

Welcome, welcome, welcome, welcome.

IN THE LOUNGE ...
GET WELL
EATING DISORDERS UNIT
EAST WING
TIFFANY
ELAINE
HI. I'M ANNA.
KATE
HEATHER
BELLA
LILY
AVA
OLIVE
PATRICK
DENZEL
CORDELIA
AL

THEN, FOR THE FIRST TIME IN YEARS, I ATE BREAKFAST . . .
LUNCH . . .
DINNER . . .

LATER THAT NIGHT . . .
I'M NOT AFRAID TO EAT NORMALLY. I DIDN'T REALIZE IT, LILY.
WELL, I'M NOT AFRAID ENOUGH! IT'S TOO EASY TO EAT AND EAT.
BUT IT'S A MYSTERY TO ME. I DON'T UNDERSTAND IT. HOW DID THE FEAR JUST STOP?
I SPOKE TO DR BISSELL, THE HOSPITAL PSYCHIATRIST.
IN TIME YOU MAY HAVE SOME ANSWERS, ANNA. PERHAPS YOU'RE FURTHER ALONG IN YOUR RECOVERY THAN YOU THINK, BUT YOU STILL HAVE A LONG WAY TO GO.
I HOPE IT'S NOT TOO FAR. IT HURTS TO EAT. I'M SO BLOATED.
YOU'RE NOT USED TO THREE MEALS A DAY. IT MAY TAKE A YEAR FOR YOUR BODY TO ADJUST.
A YEAR?
MAYBE MORE. YOUR BODY HAS TO RECOVER, TOO.
TRY NOT TO BE DISCOURAGED. AS LONG AS YOU FOLLOW YOUR FOOD PLAN, YOU'LL BEGIN TO FEEL BETTER.

FATTY FATTY
THIS ISN'T FAT!
IT'S BLOATING . . .
. . . CAUSED BY STARVING AND BINGING AND LAXATIVES AND - YOU!
ME? BUT I AM YOU AND YOU ARE ME! WE ARE THE SAME PERSON!
I'M NOT SO SURE I WANT YOU TO BE ME ANY MORE.
IT'S A LITTLE LATE FOR THAT. I'VE BEEN YOU FOR A LONG TIME AND I'M HERE TO STAY!
IT KIND OF SURPRISES ME THAT I'M FIGHTING BACK! I'M NOT AS AFRAID OF HER NOW.
WELL, THANKS A LOT!

ONE DAY, WE WERE GIVEN THE ASSIGNMENT TO PAIR OFF AND TRACE EACH OTHER'S OUTLINES ON BROWN PAPER. KATE WAS MY PARTNER.

BIRD's EYE VIEW

ANNA TRACING KATE

KATE TRACING ANNA

ANNA, YOU'RE JUST THE RIGHT SIZE, BUT I'M WAY TOO FAT!
KATE
ANNA
HUH? BUT YOUR OUTLINE IS TOO THIN!
NO! IT'S TOO FAT! I WONDER IF IT WOULD LOOK TOO FAT IF I DIDN'T KNOW IT WAS ME?
WE WERE GIVEN ANOTHER EXERCISE, TO STAND HIP TO HIP IN FRONT OF A MIRROR.
I'M WAY TOO FAT, AND YOU ARE JUST RIGHT!
WOW!

THAT NIGHT, KATE TOOK TWO HOURS TO FINISH HER DINNER, AND WE WAITED WITH HER.
COME ON, KATE!
YOU CAN DO IT.
I CAN'T! I CAN'T!
YOU CAN!
TAKE A DEEP BREATH, KATE.
KEEP TRYING.
KATE HAD HAD ANOREXIA FOR FIFTEEN YEARS. SHE WAS THIRTY YEARS OLD, AND WEIGHED SEVENTY POUNDS.
POKE
I'M JUST SO AFRAID!
WILL I EVER HAVE A LIFE?
I'VE FELT JUST LIKE THAT.
I'M SO TIRED.
WE CAN'T GIVE UP!

TYRANNY AND HER TERRIBLE, DESTRUCTIVE POWER CAME INTO FOCUS AS TIME WENT ON.

THE DAYS WERE LONG, AND WE BEGAN TO TAKE SUPERVISED WALKS IN THE NEIGHBOURHOOD.

I WAS BEGINNING TO EXPERIENCE GREAT SURGES OF THE KIND OF HAPPINESS I HAD ALMOST FORGOTTEN. I REALIZED IT WAS A SENSE OF WELL-BEING . . .

IT'S SO GOOD TO BE WRITING.
IT'S BEEN A LONG TIME.
THEN, ALL MY OLD STORIES CAME RUSHING OUT INTO THE OPEN.
YOU CAN NEVER HAVE TOO MANY DRESSES.
I JUST GOT BACK FROM THE ARCTIC!
WELL, I LOVE ICEBERG LETTUCE. DON'T YOU?
NO! CHOCOLATE!
SWEETIE!
HONEY!
WHERE'S MY HAT?
HAVE YOU FOUND THE CAR YET?
NOT YET.
I'M GETTING TIRED.
ARE WE LATE AGAIN?
THEY'LL NEVER ASK US BACK!
AND WHERE WOULD I BE WITHOUT YOU?

MORE STORIES FOLLOWED, PEOPLED BY CHARACTERS WHO HAD BEEN WAITING FOR ME ALL ALONG.
NOW WHERE IS THAT CHILD?
YOU'RE KIDDING ME, GRANDPA! I'M HERE.
HI GUYS.
ARE YOU ALL SET?
NO. I FORGOT LUNCH!
TOO LATE NOW! LET'S HURRY.
NEW YORK CITY! IT'S NOT TOO FAR.
WHERE TO?
RUN, DAD!
OH, PLEASE EAT, DEAR!
I CAN'T. I'M MUCH TOO FAT.
YOU'RE NOT.
AM I FAT?
I LOVE THE BIT IN HAMLET ... "TO THINE OWN SELF BE TRUE".
ME TOO! TOTALLY LIVE BY THAT.
CAN WE HAVE THE REPORT BY TOMORROW, CHRIS?
IF WE WORK STRAIGHT THROUGH.
YOU FOUND SHEILA!
I THINK IT'S JUST GOING TO BE TOO LONG, HONEY.
BUT IT'S ELEGANT THAT WAY!
WHERE DID YOU GET YOUR SHOES?
HEY, ED!
SAX.

A FEW DAYS BEFORE I WAS TO RETURN HOME . . .
FOUND YOUR MUSE AGAIN, I SEE.
YES, I HAVE!
HMM.
HOW BORING.
NOT FOR ME. I HAVE MY LIFE BACK. IT DOESN'T BELONG TO YOU NOW.
NO?
NO! AND I'M NOT GOING TO DO ANYTHING YOU WANT ME TO DO ANY MORE!
REALLY?

WHAT A SHAME! I MADE YOU SO THIN, AND NOW LOOK AT YOU!
YOU'RE NORMAL. HOW COULD YOU DO THAT?
PERSISTENCE. AND IT WORKED!
YOU'RE NOT POWERFUL ANY MORE.
OW.
YOU COST ME SO MUCH TIME.
BUT I THOUGHT WE WERE A TEAM!
ARE YOU FOR REAL? I COULD HAVE DIED! JUST LIKE CYNTHIA.
YOU THINK THAT'S ALL MY FAULT?

YOU FORGET ONE THING . . .
I THINK I KNOW.
I'M YOU AND YOU'RE ME!
RIGHT?
RIGHT.
BUT YOU'RE THE PART OF ME I DON'T WANT. I'LL HAVE TO BE CAREFUL THAT YOU DON'T COME BACK.
BUT . . .
YOU'D BETTER READ THIS. IT'S A LETTER I'VE BEEN WRITING TO YOU.
ME?
Tyranny,
For the first time in a long time, I have a future, and I'M HAPPY! So, once and for all, I don't care about being thin!! Goodbye, and go away!
Anna.

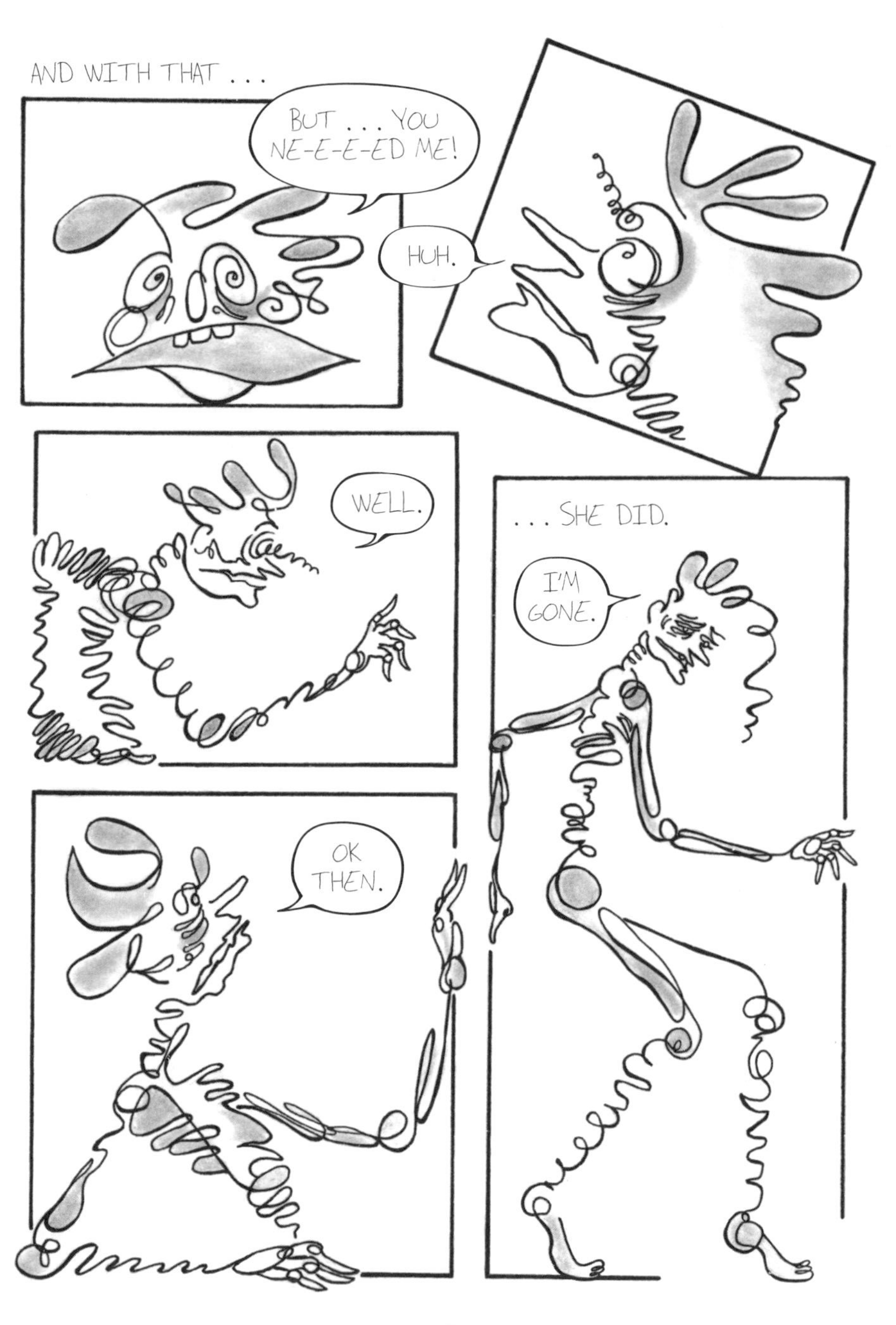
AND WITH THAT . . .
BUT . . . YOU NE-E-E-ED ME!
HUH.
WELL.
OK THEN.
. . . SHE DID.
I'M GONE.

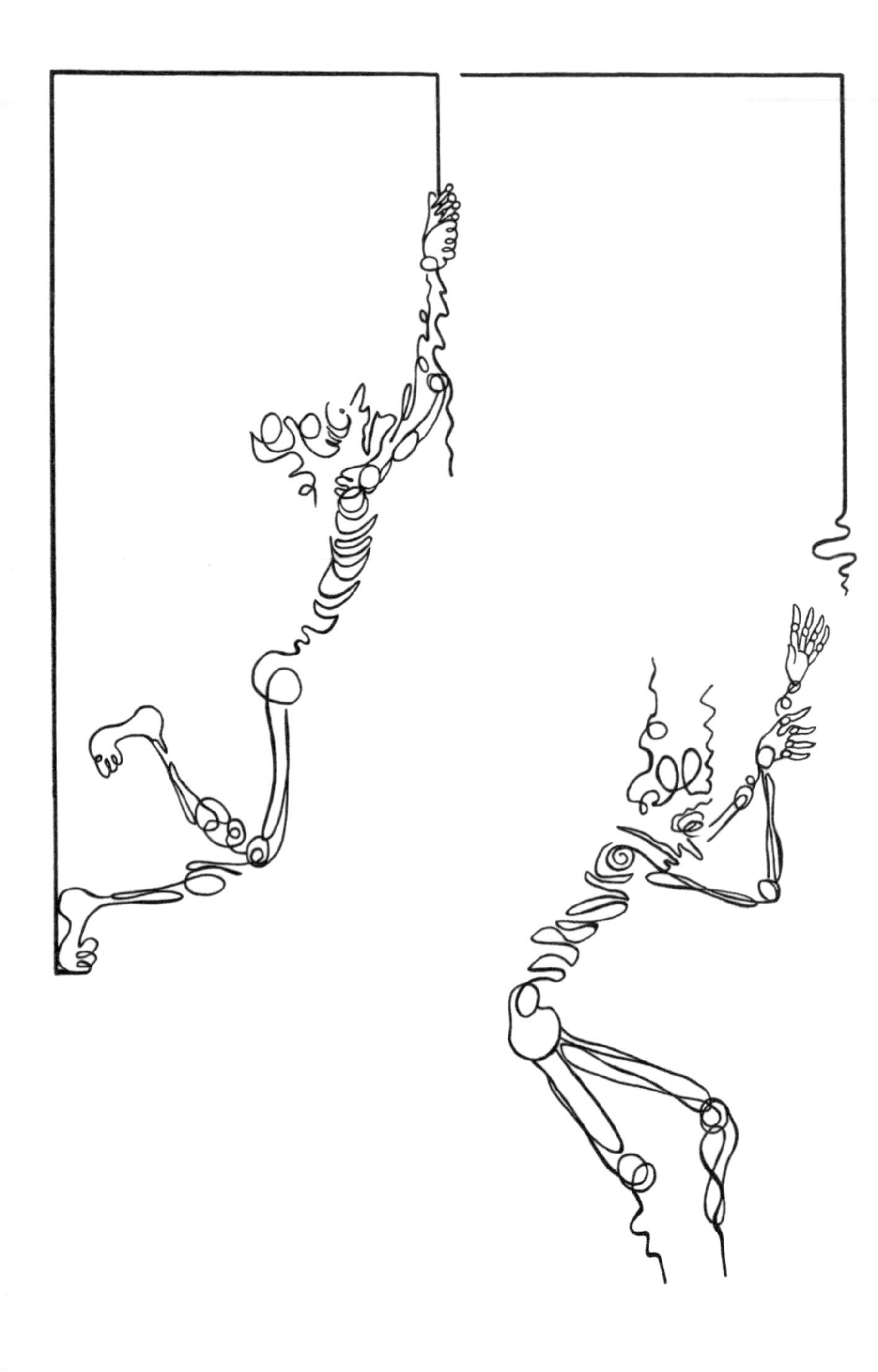

"This is one of the most moving and important

graphic novels to come along in years."

School Library Journal

"It's a powerful book: spare, probing, tough-

minded. I think this is one of the bravest books I've

encountered." Charlene Diehl, *Dig Magazine*

"Spare and unflinching ...This book could save lives."

CM Magazine

Lesley Fairfield is a graduate of the Ontario College of Art and Design and has illustrated many children's books. Her work concerning body image has appeared in *Dance in Canada* magazine and in York University's *International Women's Studies Journal*. Lesley's thirty-year battle with anorexia and bulimia has informed her work and given *Tyranny*, her first graphic novel, a sharp edge and deep insight.